"Mum, everyone's an animal."

"Don't try to talk, dear." His mother pushed him gently back onto the pillows. "The doctor will make you better."

"But the doctor's a hedgehog," Sanjay said hopelessly. Why wouldn't anyone believe him?

PETERS
FRASER
&
DUNLOP

503/4 THE CHAMBERS
CHELSEA HARBOUR
LONDON SW10 0XF

AGENT: RC
ROYALTY SHEET №: 204640100
PUBLICATION DATE: JULY 2000
CATEGORY: CHILD F

YOUNG CORGI BOOKS

Young Corgi books are perfect when you are looking for great books to read on your own. They are full of exciting stories and entertaining pictures and can be tackled with confidence. There are funny books, scary books, spine-tingling stories and mysterious ones. Whatever your interests you'll find something in Young Corgi to suit you: from ponies to football, from families to ghosts. The books are written by some of the most famous and popular of today's children's authors, and by some of the best new talents, too.

Whether you read one chapter a night, or devour the whole book in one sitting, you'll love Young Corgi books. The more you read, the more you'll want to read!

ANIMAL CRACKERS

ANIMAL CRACKERS
A YOUNG CORGI BOOK : 0 552 546267

PRINTING HISTORY
Young Corgi edition published 2000

1 3 5 7 9 10 8 6 4 2

Set in 16/20pt Bembo Schoolbook by
Phoenix Typesetting, Ilkley, West Yorkshire

Young Corgi Books are published by Transworld Publishers,
61–63 Uxbridge Road, London W5 5SA,
a division of The Random House Group Ltd,
in Australia by Random House Australia (Pty) Ltd,
20 Alfred Street, Milsons Point, Sydney NSW 2061, Australia,
in New Zealand by Random House New Zealand Ltd,
18 Poland Road, Glenfield, Auckland 10, New Zealand
and in South Africa by Random House (Pty) Ltd,
Endulini, 5a Jubilee Road, Parktown 2193, South Africa

Printed and bound in Great Britain by
Cox & Wyman Ltd, Reading, Berkshire

NARINDER DHAMI

ANIMAL CRACKERS

Illustrated by Tony Blundell

YOUNG CORGI

Sanjay's head hurt. And he was lying on a very hard bed. It was so hard, all his bones were aching. Sanjay knew that he ought to open his eyes and wake up, but he just couldn't.

"Is he all right, sir?"

Sanjay knew that voice. It was Will, his best friend. Will sounded worried. Why?

"Is he dead, sir?" That was Barry Howard. Typical.

"No, of course he isn't." And that was Mr Jackson, the headmaster. "He's just a bit dazed, that's all."

Suddenly Sanjay realized it was *him* they were talking about. He was the one who had hit his head, and he was the one feeling all dazed and confused. Now he remembered exactly what had happened, and why he was lying flat out on the hard, concrete surface of the school playground.

"Come on, give the boy some air," said Mr Jackson. "Get back to class, the lot of you. Playtime finished five minutes ago."

His eyes still closed, Sanjay heard feet shuffling reluctantly away.

"Oh, *sir*. Can't we wait and see if he's dead or not?"

"I want to see the ambulance."

"It's not fair. We never get to see the good bits."

"Sanjay?" Someone was kneeling down next to him. Sanjay struggled again to open his eyes, and this time he made it.

He looked up into the face of a polar bear wearing Mr Jackson's gold-rimmed glasses. Sanjay gasped, and closed his eyes again.

"It's all right, Sanjay," said Mr Jackson. "We've sent for an ambulance. Just take it easy."

Cautiously Sanjay opened one eye, just as Mr Jackson put a hand on his shoulder. It wasn't a hand. It was a huge, yellowy-white, furry paw.

"Mr Jackson," Sanjay said faintly. "You've turned into a polar bear."

"Don't try to speak, son." Mr Jackson looked across at someone Sanjay couldn't see. "He's hallucinating, poor kid."

"Oh dear, I wish the ambulance would hurry up." Sanjay recognized the voice of his class teacher, Miss Miller. "He could be badly hurt."

Sanjay forced himself to open his eyes again. He didn't feel too bad. He just had a bit of a headache. But he was much more interested in the fact that Mr Jackson had turned into a polar bear. The headmaster didn't seem to have noticed. Sanjay thought he'd better let him know right away.

"Sir—" he began in a stronger voice, but this time it was Miss Miller who bent over him.

"Sssh, Sanjay, don't try to talk."

Sanjay looked up at his teacher. Miss Miller was now a large, striped, tabby cat in a navy dress and sensible shoes. Sanjay gave a yelp of surprise, and closed his eyes tightly. Mr Jackson was right. He was seeing things.

"Here's the ambulance," said Mr Jackson.

Relieved, Sanjay opened his eyes again. He could see the ambulance pulling up outside the school gates. The doors opened, and a penguin and a gorilla got out.

"A penguin," Sanjay said weakly, hardly able to believe his own eyes. "And a gorilla."

"Yes, yes, dear," Miss Miller said soothingly, twitching her whiskers at him. "Just lie still."

Sanjay gave up. Feeling rather scared, he watched the penguin and the gorilla come running across the playground with a stretcher.

"This is Sanjay," Mr Jackson said to the gorilla. "He's had a bit of a bump on the head."

The gorilla knelt down.

"Hello, Sanjay," he said. "How are you feeling, son?"

"All right," Sanjay said nervously. He didn't know what else to say. The school playground was turning into London Zoo before his very eyes. "My head hurts a bit."

The gorilla quickly examined Sanjay's head with gentle paws.

"It doesn't look too bad, but we'd better get him to hospital to be checked over."

Sanjay was alarmed. He definitely didn't want to go in an ambulance with a penguin and a gorilla. He'd watched *Casualty* on the telly with his mum lots of times, and it wasn't a bit like this.

"I feel fine," he said quickly.

"Don't worry, Sanjay," said Miss Miller. "I'll come with you."

"And I'll phone your parents right away and tell them what's happened." Mr Jackson bared his teeth, which were big and sharp and yellow. Sanjay thought he was smiling, but he wasn't sure.

Sanjay felt very nervous indeed as the penguin and the gorilla lifted him onto a stretcher and carried him over to the ambulance. He felt even more nervous when he noticed that the penguin had a beard. Closing his eyes tightly, he wished and wished for everything to be back to normal. But when he opened them again, he was inside the ambulance with Miss Miller, the tabby cat, and the penguin with a beard. Then the ambulance started up, and moved off. Sanjay hoped the gorilla was a good driver.

"How are you feeling now, dear?" asked Miss Miller. She had a large, furry face with long whiskers and a pink nose, but, funnily enough, she still looked exactly like Miss Miller.

"Fine," Sanjay said. "Except that everyone's turned into an animal."

"Never mind," the penguin said cheerfully. "They'll soon sort you out at the hospital."

Sanjay could see that there was no point in going on about it, so he kept quiet. Maybe the doctors would be able to help him.

"So what happened, Sanjay?" Miss Miller asked gently. "How did you bang your head?"

Sanjay opened his mouth to say something, then closed it again. He might be seeing people turning into animals all over the place, but he wasn't stupid. He couldn't tell Miss Miller what had really happened there in the school playground, or Barry Howard would be after him.

"I slipped," he said. That was true, at least. He just wouldn't tell Miss Miller *how* he'd slipped.

"Not in a fight, were you?" asked the penguin.

Sanjay blushed.

"No," he said. That was also true. Just about.

A few minutes later they arrived at the hospital, and Sanjay began to feel much better. The ache in his head had almost gone, and the gorilla had actually been a very good driver indeed.

He was also getting quite used to the penguin with the beard by now, but he

wouldn't be sorry to get out of the
ambulance, and find a doctor who
would make him better. He liked
animals, but this was a bit much.

"Right, let's get you straight to
Casualty then, Sanjay," said the penguin.
He put Sanjay into a wheelchair and
pushed him out of the ambulance. Miss
Miller hurried after them.

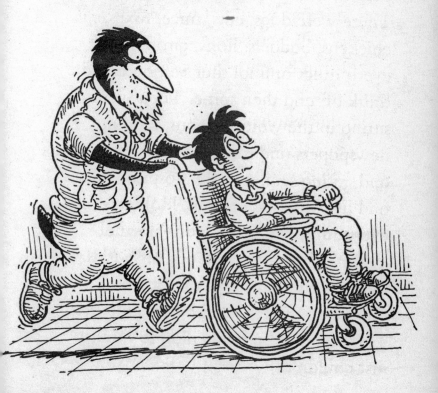

The penguin pushed Sanjay through some large glass doors and into the hospital. Sanjay was very glad indeed that he was in the wheelchair, because, if he hadn't been, he was sure he would have passed out right there on the spot.

There were animals everywhere. Wherever there should have been a person, there was an animal instead. There were dogs, cats, mice, foxes, chickens, badgers, lions, giraffes and every other animal that Sanjay could think of, and then some. They were sitting in the waiting room, reading newspapers and magazines, drinking tea and eating scones in the hospital café, and just walking around, looking as if everything was quite, quite normal.

Sanjay groaned and put his hands over his eyes, just as a rhinoceros with one leg in plaster went by on crutches. This couldn't be happening to him. It just couldn't.

Then someone walked up to them. He opened his eyes and saw a duck in a nurse's uniform.

"This is Sanjay," said the penguin. "He fell and banged his head."

"Hello, Sanjay," said the duck.

"Hello," Sanjay said politely. He'd already spoken to a polar bear, a cat, a gorilla and a penguin today, and now a duck. He was beginning to feel like Doctor Dolittle.

The nurse took Sanjay to a cubicle with a curtain round it, and helped him onto the bed. Miss Miller came too.

"The doctor will be in to see you very soon," the nurse said, and then she waddled briskly away.

Sanjay lay there and wondered what kind of animal the doctor would be. A dog? A lion? An anteater? A sudden thought struck him, and he looked down at himself. He seemed to be all right. At least *he* hadn't turned into a cat, a penguin, a polar bear or any other kind of animal.

The doctor was a hedgehog with a stethoscope round her neck. She came bustling in, and bent over Sanjay to examine him.

"How are you feeling?" she asked.

"I'm all right," Sanjay said. "But I keep seeing animals everywhere."

"How's your head?" the doctor asked, brushing her spikes off her face.

"My head's fine," Sanjay said. "It's my eyesight that's the problem."

The doctor ignored him, and looked at Miss Miller.

"We'll have to do some tests," she said. "We can't be too careful with a head injury."

"Can I have my eyes tested too?" Sanjay asked hopefully, but right at that moment the curtain was pushed back, and his mum and dad came in. Sanjay didn't know how he knew it was his mum and dad, because his mum was a hamster and his dad was a Labrador. He just knew it was them.

"Sanjay!" His mum rushed up to the bed and put a warm, furry arm round him. "What happened?"

"I fell over," Sanjay gulped. He felt a bit like crying. It was a shock to see his mum and dad looking so different.

"Is he hurt?" Sanjay's dad barked anxiously at the doctor.

"He seems all right," said the
hedgehog. "But he's got to have some
tests. I'll have a word with you in a
minute."

Dr Hedgehog went away. Sanjay sat
up and looked desperately at his mother.

"Mum, everyone's an animal."

"Don't try to talk, dear." His mother
pushed him gently back onto the
pillows. "The doctor will make you
better."

"But the doctor's a hedgehog," Sanjay said hopelessly. Why wouldn't anyone believe him?

"Yes, dear, of course she is." Sanjay's mum turned to his dad. "I think we ought to get these tests done right away. He's seeing things."

Sanjay lay back on the pillows and closed his eyes. He didn't know what else he could do.

Chapter Two

Sanjay opened his eyes and wondered
why he felt so strange. Then he
remembered. Yesterday he'd bumped his
head, and everyone had turned into
animals. Or had it all been a dream?

The doctors at the hospital had done
lots of tests, and they'd said that
everything was all right. Sanjay had tried
telling them what he was seeing, but Dr
Hedgehog had got very annoyed indeed,
and her spikes had bristled all over. So
Sanjay had just given up and kept quiet.

He'd had another shock when he got home. Not only was everyone in real life an animal, but everyone on TV was too. Sanjay had found it very strange indeed to see elephants, tigers, dogs and chimpanzees walking up and down *Coronation Street*. By the time a walrus appeared to read the news, Sanjay had had enough, and went to bed.

But today his head felt fine. Sanjay sat up in bed and rubbed his eyes. Maybe that meant everything would be back to normal, he thought hopefully. Maybe he would go downstairs and find that yesterday had just been a dream . . .

Right at that moment, a giant hamster opened Sanjay's bedroom door and walked in. Sanjay groaned and slid down under the duvet. This was no dream.

"How are you feeling, love?" his mum asked, stroking her whiskers.

"Fine," Sanjay said. He rubbed his eyes hard, even though he knew it wouldn't make a bit of difference. It didn't. When he looked again, his mum was still a hamster.

"Good." His mum smiled at him, showing her sharp little teeth. "The doctor said you'd be all right to go to school today."

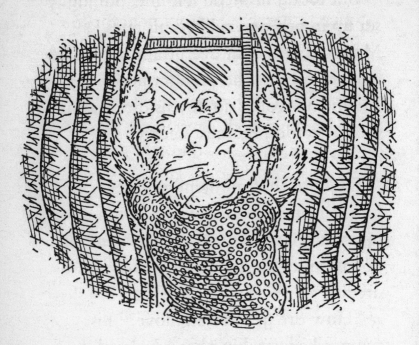

Sanjay nodded miserably. He
watched his mum opening his bedroom
curtains and wondered how anyone
couldn't know that they'd turned into a
giant furry rodent.

"Mum," he said cautiously, "do you
feel all right?"

His mum stared at him.

"Of course I do, dear."

"You don't feel a bit – well—" Sanjay stopped, searching desperately for the right word, "—*furry*?"

His mum wasn't listening. She was already halfway down the stairs.

"Hurry up and get dressed, or you won't have time for any breakfast. I'll drop you off at school on my way to work."

Sanjay rolled miserably out of bed. This was all Barry Howard's fault, he thought bitterly. If it hadn't been for Barry Howard and his gang, he wouldn't have fallen over yesterday. If he hadn't fallen over, he wouldn't have banged his head. And if he hadn't banged his head, he wouldn't be the only person left in the world who still *was* a person.

Barry Howard and his sidekicks, Ricky, Jonno and Keith, bullied most of the kids at school, but for the last few weeks Barry had been picking on

Sanjay. Sanjay had to give Barry 10p
every week, or else. Sanjay was scared
of Barry Howard, like all the kids were,
and because he got £1 pocket money
every week, 10p wasn't much to keep
Barry off his back. Barry took money
off most of the children at school, but
never more than 10p at a time, so that it
was easier for kids to pay up than to
complain. For a bully, Barry was quite
clever. That was why the teachers didn't
know what was going on.

Yesterday, though, Sanjay hadn't got
his pocket money because his mum
didn't have any change. So he hadn't
been able to pay Barry Howard
anything at all. When Barry and his

gang came up to him at playtime, Sanjay had had to say that he didn't have any money.

"What do you mean, you haven't got any money?" Barry had pushed his face right up close to Sanjay's. He had big teeth that stuck out over his lips, and his hair was shaved very short, which didn't do much for his jug-handle ears. "It's payday."

"I'll – I'll bring it tomorrow," Sanjay had squeaked. His best friend Will had been standing next to him, silent and terrified. "Honest."

"Tomorrow's no good." Barry had shaken his head slowly from side to side, staring hard at Sanjay. "I want it NOW."

When Barry had said "NOW", he had pushed his face even closer to Sanjay's, so close that Sanjay could count his freckles. Scared out of his wits, Sanjay had jumped backwards, slipped and – BANG! That was how this had all started.

"Sanjay, Will's here," his mum called from the kitchen.

Sanjay picked up his jacket and went downstairs. Sitting at the kitchen table was a shaggy sheepdog puppy. It was wearing school uniform and eating a piece of toast.

"Will?" Sanjay said doubtfully.

The sheepdog grinned at him.

"How's your head?"

"All right." Sanjay couldn't take his eyes off his friend. The sheepdog puppy had Will's face, and the same long hair that was always flopping into his eyes.

"Oh, Sanjay, you haven't got time for any breakfast," said his mum. "I told you to hurry up."

"I don't want any," Sanjay said, his eyes still fixed on Will.

"Time to go then," said Sanjay's mum, picking up her coat. "Now where have my car keys got to?"

Will got up from the table, knocking over a pot of jam and sending a buttery knife skidding to the floor.

"Oops, sorry," he said cheerfully.

Sanjay couldn't help smiling. Will was exactly like a sheepdog puppy. He was big and clumsy and awkward, and he was always knocking things over and getting in the way. When Will was a human, he even looked like a sheepdog too, with all that floppy hair and his eager expression.

Of course! All of a sudden, Sanjay realized something that he hadn't noticed before. Will was a sheepdog because that was what he was like in real life. A sheepdog. His mum was a hamster because, well, she was just like a hamster. She was neat and small and clean and tidy, always rushing here and there and never stopping, just like a hamster on its wheel. And then there was Mr Jackson, the headmaster who was now a polar bear. He *looked* round and cuddly and jolly, but he wasn't really. He could be very frightening indeed when he lost his temper. Sanjay had read somewhere that although polar bears looked cuddly, they were really quite fierce. Now Sanjay could see exactly what had happened. People hadn't become just any old animals. Everyone had become the animal they were really like. Sanjay was so amazed by what he'd discovered that he didn't realize at first that Will was whispering in his ear.

"Did you tell your mum and dad about Barry?"

"What do you think?" Sanjay whispered back. His mum was too busy looking for her car keys to take any notice of them. "I just said I slipped."

"But it was Barry's fault," Will pointed out.

Sanjay shrugged. No-one in their right mind would tell on Barry Howard. It was easier just to try and keep out of his way.

Sanjay's mum drove them to school in her car. There were animals everywhere, at the bus stop, driving past in cars and walking their children to school, but Sanjay was getting so used to it by now that he hardly noticed.

As they got closer to school, Sanjay began to wonder, for the first time, what the rest of his class would look like. What about Jamie Graham, who sat opposite him? What kind of animal would he be? Sanjay thought about it for a minute. Jamie would be a parrot, he decided, because he was always talking. Not only that, he was always trying to copy Sanjay's work. And what about Katie Lewis, who was his partner in their maths project? Katie was small and quiet, so Sanjay rather thought that she might be a mouse.

Sanjay's mum dropped them off at the school gates. As he and Will went into the playground, Sanjay looked eagerly at all the animals who were already there, doing all the things that children normally did – running around, playing football, playing skipping games and just standing in small groups, chatting. He couldn't see Jamie

Graham, but he could see a little white mouse with a skipping rope, who was definitely Katie Lewis. And wasn't that owl sitting on the wall and reading a book Farida Jalal, the brainiest girl in their class?

For the first time since yesterday, Sanjay was beginning to enjoy himself. It was good fun animal-spotting and trying to work out who was what. It was just a shame he couldn't let Will in on the joke. He'd thought about telling him, but he knew Will wouldn't believe him.

"You're a bit quiet," Will said anxiously. "Are you worried about Barry?"

Suddenly Sanjay wasn't enjoying himself any more. Instead, a horrible, cold feeling washed all over him from head to toe. How on earth had he managed to forget about Barry Howard? Of course Barry would be an animal too. The question was, what kind of animal would the terrifying Barry Howard be?

Sanjay gulped. He felt faint with fear. Why hadn't he thought about this before? If he had, he could have asked his mum to let him have the day off school. Now here he was, having to stand up to Barry Howard, who was scary enough as a human, but who would be even more frightening as an animal. And what kind of animal would Barry Howard be? A Rottweiler? A man-eating shark? A grizzly bear? And he hadn't even remembered to bring 10p with him.

Sanjay grabbed Will's arm.

"Have you got any money?" he asked in a shaky voice.

Will looked even more terrified.

"No. Did you forget the ten pence? You didn't forget the ten pence, did you?" He looked over Sanjay's shoulders and his face turned white. "Here's Barry now."

Sanjay was so scared he couldn't speak. He forced himself to turn round and find out what kind of utterly terrifying animal Barry Howard had become.

He saw four fluffy white rabbits hopping through the playground gate one by one. Three of the rabbits were Ricky,

Jonno and Keith, Barry Howard's gang.
And in front of them, in a very familiar
leather jacket, his large ears bobbing up
and down, his pink nose twitching, was
the biggest rabbit of them all.

It was Barry Howard.

Chapter Three

The whole class was doing maths, except Sanjay. Miss Miller had been very kind to him and had said, stroking her whiskers, that if he didn't feel like doing much work, he could sit quietly with a book instead. So Sanjay was sitting quietly with a book that he wasn't reading a word of because he kept staring across the classroom at Barry Howard.

Barry was in his favourite position, tipped back on two legs of his chair, his Doc Martens balanced on the edge of the table. He wasn't even pretending to do any maths. He still wore his leather jacket, and he would have looked as hard as he usually did, if it hadn't been for his long furry ears and his pink nose.

Having realized that everyone had become the animal they were really

like, Sanjay couldn't understand why
Barry Howard had turned into a rabbit.
Barry was tough. Barry was hard. Barry
could clear a classroom just by smiling.
Sanjay couldn't work it out at all.

"Sit on your chair properly, Barry," said Miss Miller wearily, for the sixth time that morning.

Barry slowly lowered his chair to the ground, his lip curled in a sneer. The sneer would have looked a bit more convincing if Barry's little pink nose hadn't been twitching like mad at the same time. Sanjay felt hysterical laughter bubbling inside him, and had to bite his lip to keep it in. He bent his head over his book and tried to read.

When Sanjay looked over at Barry again a few minutes later, he got a shock. Barry was glaring back at him. Quickly Sanjay looked away. There hadn't been time for Barry to hassle Sanjay for the 10p earlier this morning, because the lesson bell had rung the minute Barry had hopped into the playground. But Sanjay knew that Barry hadn't forgotten. Barry might be a rabbit, but he had a memory like an elephant. He would still want that 10p.

Or maybe Barry wouldn't want money, now that he was a rabbit, Sanjay thought. Maybe he would start bullying the other kids for a regular supply of carrots instead.

Sanjay smiled. He soon realized that was a mistake when he saw Barry Howard jump up and hop menacingly across the classroom towards him. Miss Miller had her back to them on the other side of the room and didn't notice, but Will, who was sitting next to Sanjay, went pale and dropped his calculator.

"Who d'you think you're staring at?"
Barry Howard stopped in front of
Sanjay, and glared at him.

Sanjay was dying to answer "Bugs
Bunny", but didn't dare.

"No-one," he said.

Barry's nose twitched furiously.

"We've got some business to sort out
at playtime," he said threateningly.

Well, it was meant to be threatening, but Sanjay was too mesmerized by the long, furry ears bobbing about on Barry's head to take any notice.

"Barry Howard," called Miss Miller. "What are you doing out of your seat?"

"I need something from the maths cupboard, Miss," Barry called back.

Miss Miller sighed.

"If you ever did any maths, Barry, I might believe you. Go and sit down."

Barry grinned nastily, showing large buck teeth.

"Playtime," he hissed at Sanjay, and hopped away. Sanjay wanted to laugh again as he watched Barry's cotton wool tail bobbing across the classroom.

"What're you smiling for, Sanjay?" Will groaned. "This is serious."

"Mm," said Sanjay. It was no good. He couldn't take a rabbit in a leather jacket seriously, however hard he tried.

"We'll have to try and borrow ten

pence from someone," Will said anxiously.

Sanjay looked thoughtful. He couldn't see any reason at all why he should give money to a rabbit.

"Maybe."

"Maybe?" Will repeated, appalled.

"Let's just wait and see what happens," Sanjay said carefully.

Will buried his head in his arms.

"I know what'll happen," he said. "And it won't be nice."

"We'll see," Sanjay said. After all, how scary could a bunch of rabbits be? He found out at playtime. As he and Will went out into the playground, they were immediately surrounded by a battalion of bunnies, and hustled off to Barry's lair. This was a deserted corner of the playground where Barry always took his victims, out of sight of the teachers on duty. They were followed by a large group of children, who pretended to be playing football or other games a safe distance away, so that they could watch what was going on.

Barry, Ricky, Jonno and Keith stood round Sanjay and Will in a furry circle, so that they were trapped. Will looked scared, but Sanjay wasn't. He'd never been frightened of white rabbits, and he wasn't going to start now.

"Where's my ten pence?" Barry Howard demanded, hopping right up to them. He hopped so close that Sanjay could count Barry's whiskers. But this time Sanjay did not back away. "Hand it over."

"I haven't got it," Sanjay said, again trying not to laugh. When Barry was being hard, his little nose twitched like mad.

"So you think I'm gonna let you off, just because you banged your head yesterday," Barry jeered, winking at the rest of his gang. His long ears bobbed up and down, and Sanjay bit down hard on his lip.

"Hey, wait a minute," said Ricky, who was a small, plump rabbit with spectacles. "He's laughing at you, Bazza!"

There was an appalled gasp from the watching children, who now weren't even pretending to be playing games. Sanjay fought desperately to keep a straight face.

"You laughing at me?" Barry grabbed the front of Sanjay's sweatshirt with a furry paw.

"N-n-no." Sanjay could hardly get the word out. If only Barry's nose would stop twitching, he'd be all right. He wasn't going to laugh. *He wasn't.*

"You are." Barry bared his teeth.

"I'm not," Sanjay insisted faintly.

"You are!" Barry's nose twitched like crazy.

Suddenly Sanjay couldn't stand it a minute longer. He was having an argument with a rabbit in a leather jacket, and he just had to laugh. He burst into giggles. Once he'd started he couldn't stop.

"Shut up!" yelled Barry, clenching his paws.

Sanjay took one look at him, and laughed even more. He laughed and laughed until his sides were sore.

When Sanjay finally stopped laughing, there was a dreadful silence, and Barry Howard's furry face was purple with rage. Sanjay wondered, quite calmly, what Barry was going to do now. But before anyone could say anything, the lesson bell rang out, breaking the silence.

"I'll get you for this," Barry Howard snarled at Sanjay.

Then he turned and hopped away.

Chapter Four

After playtime, Sanjay's class did different things. Some children carried on with their maths, some started writing stories and others were painting pictures. Barry Howard was one of the children who were supposed to be finishing off their maths, but Sanjay knew exactly what Barry was really doing. Barry was planning exactly how he was going to get his revenge on Sanjay for laughing at him.

"Why did you have to go and *laugh* at him?" Will wailed quietly for the twentieth time. He and Sanjay were supposed to be writing a story together, but they hadn't got very far. "You know what he's like. He's going to sort you out."

Sanjay didn't answer. He wasn't really listening to Will. He was thinking,

trying to work out why tough guy
Barry Howard had become a rabbit in
this strange new world.

If Barry was a rabbit now, that meant
he was like a rabbit in real life, Sanjay
reasoned. That meant Barry wasn't
really tough and hard and frightening.
Underneath it all, he was just a coward.
A rabbit.

Sanjay grinned triumphantly as he
finally worked this out. Unfortunately
he also looked up at the same moment,
and saw Barry glaring at him. Barry
immediately drew his furry paw menacingly
across his throat. Will saw it too, and he
turned pale.

"We've got to do something," he said
urgently to Sanjay, and put his hand up.
Miss Miller came over to see what he
wanted.

"Yes, Will?" She looked down at the
blank sheets of paper on their table. "Oh
dear, you haven't got very far with your
story, have you, boys?"
"Me and Sanjay were wondering if

you need any help at lunchtime, Miss,"
Will said eagerly. "We could stay in and
tidy the bookshelves."

Miss Miller was already shaking her
head.

"Thank you, Will, but the teachers
are having a staff meeting at lunchtime,
so the classroom will be locked. Now
get on with your work, please."

Will looked upset as Miss Miller went
off.

"If we could have stayed in at lunchtime,
we could've kept away from Barry."

Sanjay shrugged.

"What's the point? Even if I kept out
of Barry's way today, he'd still get me
tomorrow."

"Aren't you scared?" Will asked
curiously.

Sanjay looked across at Barry
Howard, the bully who'd become a
rabbit. He shook his head.

"Not any more," he said.

The classroom clock ticked round to lunchtime. Every time Sanjay looked up and caught Barry's eye, Barry grinned nastily at him, and tapped his watch. Sanjay knew that whatever Barry was going to do, it was going to happen at lunchtime. He felt a bit nervous, but he didn't feel scared.

The bell rang out at exactly twelve o'clock. Barry and his gang immediately leapt up and disappeared out of the door, all grinning and showing rows of buck teeth as big as tombstones. Sanjay got up slowly and put his papers and pens away, knowing that they would be waiting for him outside.

"We'd better stay close to the dinner ladies," said Will, who was hovering anxiously round him.

"You wait for me in the playground," Sanjay said suddenly. "I've got to get something from the cloakroom."

Will frowned, but went. Everyone

else had gone too, and Sanjay was left alone in the classroom. He walked slowly out and went down the corridor to the cloakroom. He didn't really have anything to get at all. He just wanted to get rid of Will before the big bust-up with Barry Howard. He didn't think it was fair to drag his best friend into it.

There was a long mirror on the
cloakroom wall, hanging next to the
rows and rows of coats on pegs. Sanjay
looked at his face in it. For some reason,
he hadn't turned into an animal himself.
He was still the same old Sanjay. But if
he *had* become an animal, what kind of
animal would he be?

Sanjay looked long and hard at his
slightly pointed face. What was he like?
He was quite clever, often top of his

class, and he was quick and agile. He was good at games, especially climbing and running. In fact, now that he thought about it, he was cleverer and smarter than Barry and all his gang, and he could run faster too. Why had he never realized all this before?

Maybe, just maybe, Sanjay thought, he might have been a fox. A clever, wily fox, who could run fast and outsmart everyone. And a fox could easily catch a rabbit . . .

Bright sunshine hit Sanjay full in the
face when he stepped out into the
playground. It blinded him for a couple
of seconds, and in those seconds he was
swiftly surrounded by Barry's bunnies.

"Right, you." Barry poked Sanjay in
the chest with his paw. "I'm gonna
teach you a lesson."

Sanjay thought fast. He had to come
up with a plan quickly. For a minute his

mind went blank. Then his brain started working again, and he decided exactly what he was going to do.

"What lesson?" he asked calmly.

"You're going to be my slave." Barry was grinning all over his rabbity face. He was enjoying himself. "You're going to do my sums in class, you're going to give me your packed lunch every day and you're going to do my homework. You're going to do *whatever* I say."

"No way," Sanjay said firmly.

"Yes, you are!" Barry gritted his teeth. "Or else."

Sanjay shrugged.

"No," he said.

This was a new one on Barry. He stared uncertainly at Sanjay, and then at his gang.

"You'll have to *make* him do it, Bazza," said Jonno.

"Yeah. Right," Barry mumbled. He turned back to Sanjay, with a sneer.

"You'd better do it, or I'll *make* you."

Sanjay shook his head.

"I won't," he said.

There was a moment's stunned silence. Then Jonno muttered, "Let's get him, Bazza," and the rabbits began to shuffle forward menacingly.

Sanjay seized his chance. He dropped to his knees and shot right through the middle of Barry's bandy legs, bowling Barry right over onto his backside.

Then Sanjay picked himself up, and ran for it.

Chapter Five

Sanjay heard furious shouts behind him,
but he didn't stop. He had already
worked out which way he was going,
and he disappeared smartly round the
back of the school. Some of the children
in the playground had realized what
was going on, had stopped their games
and were watching, open-mouthed.

Sanjay knew that none of them would give him away – unless Barry bullied them into it. So he had to be ready for that, and think ahead.

There were several doors standing open along the back of the school. Sanjay dived through the nearest one, and tiptoed quietly down the corridor.

"Where'd he go?" he heard Barry roaring outside. Then Jonno yelling, "We'd better split up."

Sanjay grinned. That suited him perfectly.

He stopped outside his own classroom door and took a quick look through the glass. Miss Miller was still inside, collecting up her papers ready for the staff meeting. Then Sanjay glanced back down the corridor. Jonno had just come through the door and was searching the cloakrooms.

Quickly Sanjay knocked loudly on the classroom door, and then hid behind a handy bookcase. The timing was perfect. Miss Miller appeared at the classroom door, just as Jonno reached it himself.

"What are you doing in here, Jonathan?" snapped Miss Miller. "You know the rules about coming into school at lunchtime. And why did you knock on the classroom door?"

"I didn't, Miss." Jonno sounded puzzled. Behind the bookcase, Sanjay smiled.

Miss Miller looked even more annoyed.

"Some silly joke, I suppose. I think you'd better go up to the detention room right away."

"But, Miss, I haven't had my lunch yet," whined Jonno.

"Really," said Miss Miller grimly. "Well, if you're going to be so childish, I think you'd better go and have lunch with the Infants. Come along."

Sanjay smiled even more. Lunch with the Infants was not a pleasant experience. Some of them didn't yet know what a knife and fork were for.

"But, Miss!" Jonno wailed. His protests got fainter and fainter, until Sanjay couldn't hear anything at all. Then he stepped out from behind the bookcase, and looked up and down the empty corridor.

The fox had managed to catch a rabbit. One down, three to go.

Sanjay ran back out into the playground. All the children there stopped playing, and stared at him, wide-eyed with fear.

"Barry's looking for you," said one of them, a black-and-white kitten, breathlessly.

Sanjay nodded.

"Anyone seen Ricky or Keith?" he asked. He didn't want Barry yet. Barry was for later.

"Ricky's gone round the front of the school," said the kitten.

Sanjay ran round to the other side of the playground. Ricky was patrolling up and down the playground gates, as if he were a policeman. He hadn't noticed Sanjay yet.

Sanjay hurried over to the nearest

dinner lady, a dormouse in a blue
overall.

"Excuse me, Miss," he said politely.
"Miss Miller wants to see Ricky Bell
right away."

"Oh, right," said the dinner lady. She
shaded her eyes with her hand and

looked round the playground. "I can't see him anywhere."

"There he is," said Sanjay. He waved his arm in the air and yelled, "Hey! Ricky!"

Ricky looked over, then jumped backwards as if he couldn't believe his eyes. He charged across the playground towards Sanjay as fast as he could hop, knocking kids out of the way like skittles. Sanjay waited calmly next to the dinner lady.

"Miss Miller wants to see you, Ricky," the dinner lady said, when Ricky skidded to a halt in front of her.

Ricky glared at Sanjay, obviously dying to grab him and march him off to find Barry. But he couldn't with the dinner lady standing there.

"Who says?" he demanded rudely.

"I do," snapped the dinner lady. "Off you go."

Ricky looked suspiciously at Sanjay.

"I bet she doesn't really want to see me—" he began.

"Did you hear what I said?" the dinner lady squeaked at him. "Now off you go, before you get a detention!"

Ricky threw Sanjay a look of disgust, and went. Sanjay breathed a sigh of relief. Another rabbit caught in his trap. But there was still Keith to get rid of, and then the big one. Barry himself.

A hand fell on Sanjay's shoulder, and he almost jumped out of his skin. Luckily it was only Will.

"What's going on?" Will gasped, shaking his shaggy fringe out of his eyes.

"Barry Howard and all his gang are looking everywhere for you!"

Sanjay grinned.

"Not all of them," he said. "Ricky's on his way to see Miss Miller, and Jonno's having lunch with the Infants."

"What's going on?" Will looked puzzled.

"Tell you later," Sanjay hissed. He'd just spotted Keith hopping out of the canteen, and looking round. "This is what I want you to do."

Sanjay whispered quickly in Will's ear, and then disappeared round the back of the school again.

"Hey, Keith!" Will shouted. "If you're looking for Sanjay, he went that way!" And Will pointed to the back of the school, in the direction which Sanjay had gone.

"Yeah, right," said Keith scornfully. "D'you think I'm stupid or something?"

"But he *did* go that way!" Will insisted, trying not to laugh.

Keith glared at him.

"You don't fool me," he snapped.

"Please yourself." Will shrugged. "Sanjay didn't go anywhere near the – er – teachers' cars, you know."

Keith grinned.

"Sure," he said, and hopped away in the opposite direction towards the teachers' car park, which was right over the other side of the playground.

Sanjay, who was watching from round the side of the school, gave Will a thumbs-up. It would take Keith a long time to look all round the car park.

Ricky was kicking his heels outside the
classroom waiting for Miss Miller,
who'd gone to a staff meeting, and
Jonno was getting covered in custard by
screaming five-year-olds.

Now it was time to trap the biggest
rabbit of all.

Sanjay went round the back of the
school to look for Barry. He didn't have
long to wait. As Sanjay walked round
the corner, Barry suddenly hopped out
of one of the other doors further along

the building. He didn't see Sanjay, but hopped off in the opposite direction.

"Over here, Barry," Sanjay called.

The watching children froze as Barry spun round. Immediately Sanjay began to walk towards him, timing his steps carefully. He had to get this right, because he had only one chance.

Barry was hopping furiously towards him. So Sanjay walked a little bit faster. They reached each other at exactly the place Sanjay had been hoping for.

"Right, you!" shouted Barry. "You're for it, you are!"

"You mean I've got to be your slave?" Sanjay asked loudly.

"Yeah, you *and* that stupid friend of yours!" Barry roared. "And forget about those ten pences every week. You can give me *twenty* pence from now on."

"That's not fair," said Sanjay. "What about all the other kids you take money off every week?"

"Yeah, they can pay twenty pence as well." Barry shouted. "You can all pay twenty pence from now on!" He pointed furiously at the huge crowd of children who'd now silently gathered to watch what was happening, Will amongst them.

"No, make it fifty pence!"

The children gasped, outraged.

"Did you say fifty pence?" Sanjay asked. "You  mean we all have to pay you fifty pence a week?"

"You heard what I said!" Barry
yelled, his face bright red. "Fifty pence
every week on the dot or else!"

"Or else what?" said the stern voice of
the headmaster just above their heads.

Sanjay glanced up. He could just see Barry's horrified face out of the corner of his eye. Barry hadn't realized that they were standing just underneath the windows of the headmaster's office. Barry hadn't noticed that the windows were open, nor had he remembered that today there was a staff meeting, so that all the teachers and Mr Jackson were sure to be in there. Mr Jackson, looking very angry indeed, was standing at the windows, staring down at them. Behind him in a circle stood all the other teachers. Miss Miller was one of them, and she looked just as angry.

Sanjay glanced across at Barry, who, shoulders sagging, now looked like a large balloon that was rapidly deflating.

"Come up and see me right away, Barry," said Mr Jackson, leaning out of the window and fixing Barry with his beady, black polar-bear eyes. "You and I have got a lot to talk about."

Sanjay watched as Barry Howard hopped dismally and silently into school.

He suddenly realized that he was out of
breath, and that his knees were
wobbling. Then he heard the children
cheering and shouting, and wondered
what was going on. He only grasped the
fact that *he* was the one being cheered
when a great wave of children, Will at
the front, rushed forward and swamped
him.

"Excellent!" gasped Will. "Well done, Sanjay! You really sorted Barry out."

He reached out and slapped Sanjay on the back. Sanjay stumbled, and lost his footing in the crowd of cheering children. The last thing he remembered was falling heavily to the ground . . .

Chapter Six

Sanjay's head hurt, and he was lying on a very hard bed. It was so hard, all his bones were aching . . .

Hang on a minute, Sanjay thought. I've been here before.

His eyes snapped open. He was once again lying on the hard surface of the playground with a crowd of people around him. *People?*

"Come on, you lot, off you go to
lunch," Mr Jackson was saying sternly.
He was looking anxiously down at
Sanjay, his round face full of concern.
"Dear me, you seem to be making a bit
of a habit of this, Sanjay."

Sanjay gazed up at him. The polar
bear had vanished, and Mr Jackson
was Mr Jackson again. Sanjay looked
round.

Miss Miller was there, the real Miss Miller, not the tabby cat, and Will with his sheepdog fringe, but he  wasn't a sheepdog any more.

 Sanjay smiled. "You're all people again," he said. Then a sudden, horrible thought struck him, and he struggled to sit up. "All that stuff with Barry . . . I didn't dream it, did I?"

Will, who was still hanging round although the other children had gone, grinned and shook his head.

"You leave Barry Howard to me," said Mr Jackson grimly.

Sanjay sighed with relief.

"That's all right then," he said happily.

"Here's the ambulance," said Miss Miller. Sanjay hoped it was the penguin and the gorilla in the ambulance again. It was, except that they were now people.

"Why don't you try breaking your leg or cracking a rib next time, for a bit of a change?" joked the short, bearded man who had been a penguin, as they put Sanjay on a stretcher.

"I won't be doing this again," Sanjay said firmly. He didn't know what had happened to him over the last few days, but he didn't care. His world was now back to normal, but without the menace of Barry Howard. It had all been worth it.

As the two men lifted him into the ambulance, Sanjay caught sight of his reflection in the window. He blinked, surprised.

Just for a second, he had thought he was looking at the long ears and slanting eyes of a fox's face.

THE END

SAMMY'S SUPER SEASON
Lindsay Camp

A cat who can play football?!

Harry's cat, Sammy, is no ordinary tabby – he's the star goalkeeper of the school football team. And it's not just Harry and his school-mates who are fans. Sammy's spectacular saves attract the attention of Mudchester United FC. Will Sammy be tempted to play in the Premiership, or would he rather be at home eating Katbix?

A very funny story about an amazing footballing cat – perfect for building reading confidence.

0 552 546615

Books to get your teeth into

YOUNG CORGI